D1441504

Mary Had a Little Lamb

Retold by MEGAN BORGERT-SPANIOL

Illustrated by IRISZ AGOCS

CANTATA
LEARNING
MANKATO, MINNESOTA

CANTATA
LEARNING
MANKATO, MINNESOTA

Published by Cantata Learning
1710 Roe Crest Drive
North Mankato, MN 56003
www.cantatalearning.com

Library of Congress Control Number: 2014938331
ISBN: 978-1-63290-070-8

Mary Had Little a Lamb retold by Megan Borgert-Spaniol
Illustrated by Irisz Agocs

Book design by Tim Palin Creative
Music produced by Wes Schuck
Audio recorded, mixed, and mastered at Two Fish Studios, Mankato, MN

Printed in the United States of America.

VISIT
WWW.CANTATALEARNING.COM/ACCESS-OUR-MUSIC

A lamb is a baby sheep. It is covered in soft **wool**.
Most lambs stay near their mom as they **graze** and play.
But the little lamb in this song wants to be with Mary!

When you hear the lamb, turn the page.

Mary had a little lamb,
Little lamb, little lamb.

Mary had a little lamb,
Its **fleece** was white as snow.

And everywhere that Mary went,
Mary went, Mary went.

Everywhere that Mary went,
The lamb was sure to go.

It followed her to school one day,
School one day, school one day.

It followed her to school one day,
Which was against the rules.

It made the children laugh and play,
Laugh and play, laugh and play.

It made the children laugh and play,
To see a lamb at school.

And so the teacher turned it out,
Turned it out, turned it out.

And so the teacher turned it out,
But still it **lingered** near.

It waited patiently about,
Patiently about, patiently about.

It waited patiently about,
Until she did appear.

"Why does the lamb love Mary so,
Mary so, Mary so?

Why does the lamb love Mary so?"
the **eager** children cried.

"Mary loves the lamb, you know,
lamb, you know, the lamb, you know.

Yes, Mary loves the lamb, you know,"
the teacher did reply.

GLOSSARY

eager—excited

fleece—a sheep's wool coat

graze—to feed on grass and other plants

lingered—stayed for a while

wool—the thick, soft hair that grows on sheep

Mary Had a Little Lamb

Public Domain
Traditional

Piano

TO LEARN MORE

Blair, Eric. *The Boy Who Cried Wolf: A Retelling of Aesop's Fable*. Mankato, MN: Picture Window Books, 2012.

Longenecker, Theresa. *Who Grows Up on the Farm?: A Book About Farm Animals and Their Offspring.* Minneapolis: Picture Window Books, 2003.

Reasoner, Charles. *Little Bo Peep*. North Mankato, MN: Picture Window Books, 2014.

Schubert, Leda. *Feeding the Sheep*. New York: Farrar, Straus and Giroux, 2010.

White, Mark. *The Wolf in Sheep's Clothing: A Retelling of Aesop's Fable*. Mankato, MN: Picture Window Books, 2012.